TAKE YOUR TIME

To Robert Furrow, naturalist extraordinaire.
Love, Eva and Mamma

To Jack and Peter with much love.
And to Ginger, my wonderful agent and friend
who always makes me laugh. You are the BEST! —LM

Henry Holt and Company
Publishers since 1866
175 Fifth Avenue
New York, New York 10010
mackids.com

Library of Congress Cataloging-in-Publication Data
Names: Furrow, Eva, author. | Napoli, Donna Jo, 1948– author. | Molk, Laurel, illustrator.
Title: Take your time : a tale of Harriet, the Galapagos tortoise / Eva Furrow and Donna Jo Napoli ; illustrated by Laurel Molk.
Description: First edition. | New York : Henry Holt and Company, 2017. | Summary: "A tortoise from the Galapagos Islands goes on an
adventure—at her own speed"— Provided by publisher.
Identifiers: LCCN 2016002262 | ISBN 9780805095210 (hardback)
Subjects: | CYAC: Galapagos tortoise—Fiction. | Turtles—Fiction. | Animals—Galapagos Islands—Fiction. | Speed—Fiction. | Self-acceptance—
Fiction. | Galapagos Islands—Fiction. | BISAC: JUVENILE FICTION / Animals / General. | JUVENILE FICTION / Social Issues / New
Experience. | JUVENILE FICTION / Nature & the Natural World / General (see also headings under Animals).
Classification: LCC PZ7.F9665915 Tak 2017 | DDC (E)—dc23
LC record available at https://lccn.loc.gov/2016002262

Our books may be purchased in bulk for promotional, educational, or business use. Please contact your local bookseller or the Macmillan
Corporate and Premium Sales Department at (800) 221-7945 ext. 5442 or by e-mail at MacmillanSpecialMarkets@macmillan.com.

First Edition—2017 / Designed by Eileen Savage
The illustrations for this book were created with watercolor and block prints, enhanced digitally.
Printed in China by RR Donnelley Asia Printing Solutions Ltd.,
Dongguan City, Guangdong Province

1 3 5 7 9 10 8 6 4 2

APR 06 2017

TAKE YOUR TIME

A Tale of Harriet, the Galápagos Tortoise

by **EVA FURROW**
and **DONNA JO NAPOLI**

illustrated by
LAUREL MOLK

Henry Holt and Company
New York

Harriet did everything slowly.

She smelled the papayas and swamp hibiscus.
All morning.

She munched cactus pads and apples.
All afternoon.

She slumbered deep. All night.
Yes, Harriet did everything slowly.

The other animals scolded her.

"Your rhythm's all wrong, Harriet."

"It's a matter of timing. Your timing's off."

"Life in the fast track is exciting."

"The way you move, you can't go anywhere."

"You don't know what you're missing!"

Harriet calmly yawned and fell asleep.
But in the morning, she was curious.
What was she missing?

Harriet decided to go out into the big world. She wanted to see the penguin parade on a neighboring island. It took place in summer.

To get there on time, Harriet left in winter, the rainy season. She was in no hurry. There was plenty to see along the way.

She swam past hammerhead sharks.
She swam past humpback whales.
She swam past giant rays.
What wonderful things the sea held.

The penguins were delighted that she made it just in time.

While she was there, Harriet offered little
iguanas a ride through the dunes.
She walked past pink flamingos.
She walked past blue-footed boobies.
She walked past red-throated frigate birds.
What wonderful things the sky held.

The ride took months and months. By the end, the little iguanas were big iguanas, big enough to scoot off on their own.

Now the rainy season had come
again. Harriet dug a hole to make a
pool for the sea lions. While she worked, other
friends filled the pool.
    She dug past crawly centipedes.
    She dug past slippery snakes.
    She dug past skittery crabs.
    What wonderful things the earth held.

Harriet stood back and looked at the wide, deep pool.
Another whole year had passed. Maybe it was time to
go home.

Harriet swam steadily, day after day,

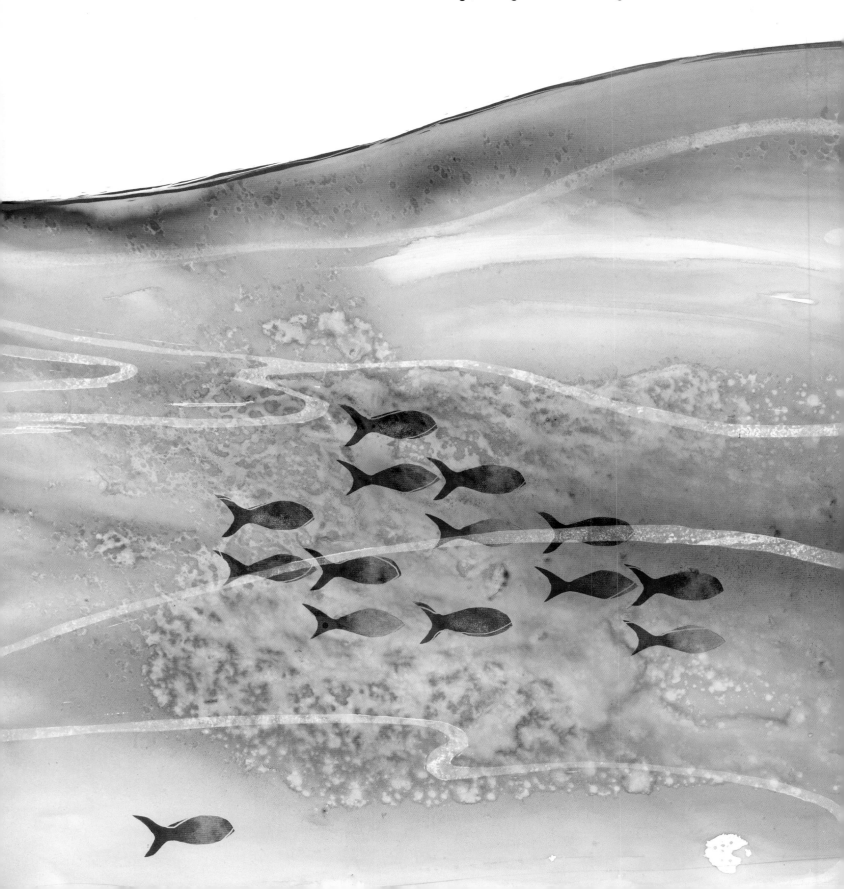

week after week,

month after month.

She was just about to crawl up onto her home shore when a pod of playful dolphins circled her.

"Been out traveling, have you? Imagine how much farther you could go if you went fast. Come on—take a chance. You won't believe how good speed is."

Harriet was spellbound by their quick grace.
When the largest dolphin offered his back,
she clung to it.

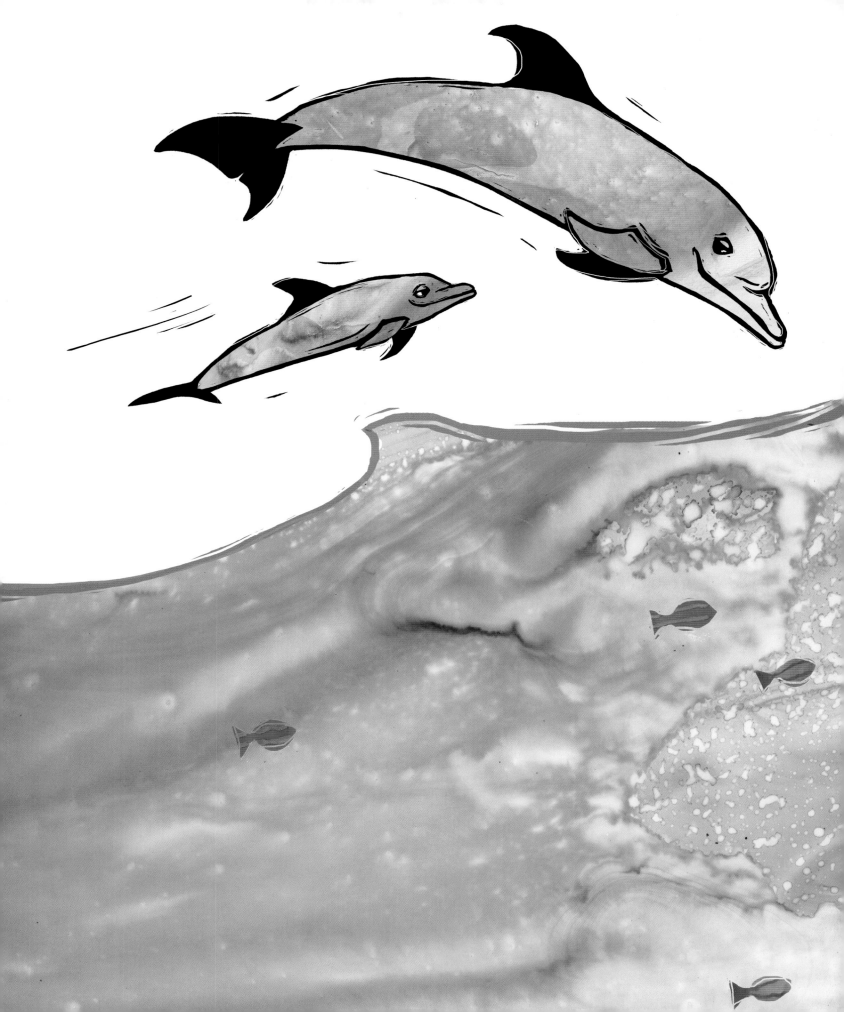

She was pulled out into the swirling current.
Moving so fast was thrilling. Look how far they
had gone in an instant!

But the wind seared, so she had to close
her eyes. And the water whooshed through
her nostrils until all she could taste was salt.
The thrill passed.

Harriet let go, and the dolphins raced ahead. Slowly, she swam home, savoring the cool spray, the rhythm of the waves, the reflection of the sun on the water.

It took her five hours, but what glorious hours.

Harriet thought about all the creatures she had
seen moving in the sea and the sky and the earth.

Sharks could cruise or whisk along fast.

Boobies clumped clumsily on land but soared in the air.

Snakes wiggled side to side, so you sometimes didn't even know where they were headed.

But slow or fast, clumsy or graceful, straight or wiggly, everyone had a rhythm that worked.

Isn't that nice?

Harriet burrowed into the grasses—
and took her own sweet time.

AUTHORS' NOTE

Harriet was the name of a real giant Galápagos tortoise. She is believed to have been collected from the Galápagos Islands (a set of sixteen islands and many smaller islets about six hundred miles to the west of Ecuador) and was eventually brought to Australia in the mid 1800s. She lived in Steve Irwin's Australia Zoo outside of Brisbane.

She liked yellow. She ate carrots, spinach, papayas, and apples and grazed on grasses, cactus pads, and flowers. She liked being tickled on her hind legs and tail and being patted on her scutes (the horny plates covering her shell). When she was scared, she pulled herself totally inside her shell. If she got turned over, she groaned as she righted herself. She often burrowed in grass.

When she died on June 23, 2006, at the estimated age of 175, she was the world's oldest animal in captivity.

On the Internet, you can find photos and videos of giant Galápagos tortoises swimming and walking. People used to think they were poor swimmers until sightings of them far out in the ocean were reported.

The giant Galápagos tortoise was hunted for many years and is close to extinction. Those remaining on the islands are now protected by law.